The Masterwork of a Painting Elephant

THE Masterwork

OF A Painting Elephant

MICHELLE CUEVAS

Pictures by
ED YOUNG

Frances Foster Books
Farrar Straus Giroux
New York

Text copyright © 2011 by Michelle Cuevas
Pictures copyright © 2011 by Ed Young
Distributed in Canada by D&M Publishers, Inc.
Printed in September 2011 in the United States of America
by RR Donnelley & Sons Company, Crawfordsville, Indiana
Designed by Lilian Rosenstreich
First edition, 2011
1   3   5   7   9   10   8   6   4   2

mackids.com

Library of Congress Cataloging-in-Publication Data
Cuevas, Michelle.
    The masterwork of a painting elephant / Michelle Cuevas. — 1st ed.
        p.   cm.
    Summary: Pigeon Jones, abandoned as a baby, is found and raised by Birch, a white,
former circus elephant who paints beautiful pictures, and through their travels and
adventures they discover the meanings of love and family.
    ISBN: 978-0-374-34854-0
    [1. Orphans—Fiction.   2. Elephants—Fiction.   3. Artists—Fiction.
4. Voyages and travels—Fiction.   5. Love—Fiction.]   I. Title.

PZ7.C89268Mas 2011
[Fic]—dc22

                                                                    2010033108

For all the Birches in my life,
my parents in particular

Contents

The Masterwork of a Painting Elephant

ONE

But He Has Such Big Ears

My name is Pigeon Jones, and I was raised by a painting Indian elephant. This is how my adventure started: one day when I was an infant in my crib, a pigeon flew into our house through the window. This is not, as you may be thinking, why I am named Pigeon. The bird did, however, cause my mama to become quite upset.

"Get that filthy bird out of here," she shouted. "Don't let it touch the baby."

My papa didn't see the bird at first, but he stayed calm, sat still, and whispered under his breath, "Just be quiet now. Wait till she lands."

The pigeon was fat. And clumsy. She landed on the side of my crib and flapped her wings so hard she got tangled in the solar-system mobile overhead. Several planets went flying. Venus fell into my crib with a thud and missed my head by only a few inches.

My mama screamed, "Grab that stupid bird."

The bird didn't seem to mind being called stupid, and when Papa approached, she climbed onto his outstretched arm one foot at a time.

Papa put the bird on a tree branch outside the window, and that crazy bird began to sing. Loudly. And not very well.

My mama and papa came over and stared down at me. The sun filtered through the leaves on the tree and dappled the light, making continents on my skin. I wasn't crying. In truth I was enjoying the show from my crib.

"The baby kept calm through the entire commotion," Papa said thoughtfully. "Through the flapping and the flying and a planet almost falling on his head. I wonder if he can hear?"

"But he has such big ears," Mama gasped. "How could anyone not hear with those enormous ears?" It was true. I had ridiculously big ears. Huge. Gigantic. They looked like someone had taken dinner plates and attached them to the sides of my head. I was, in this way, quite unlike my parents, who both

had remarkably small ears. I think this made it hard for them to hear each other, so they'd end up yelling most of the time.

But the doctor confirmed that there was nothing at all wrong with my big ears. My papa got more and more interested in the way the world looked and sounded to me, such a calm and unconcerned baby. Every time he heard or saw something interesting, he'd say, "I wonder how the baby"—they hadn't yet given me a name—"would sense that?" and write it down. He had long lists all over the house describing things like how it sounds when someone steps on dry leaves or when a dog laps water or the unexpected noise when a child's toy drops in the next room. His plan was to ask me all these things as soon as I was old enough to talk. Of course, as with many plans in life, by the time I could talk, most of the lists would have turned yellow and been forgotten.

And if you think my papa sounds a bit strange, then you've never had the pleasure of meeting my mama. After I was born she became possessed by a heart-racing, hand-wringing sense of worry that something awful might befall me.

"He'll get eaten by a tiger," she'd cry. "Or hit by a bus.

I just know it." She had daily panic attacks and would have to put her head between her legs and breathe into a paper bag.

She worried and worried, until one day, overcome by tears, she was sent to bed for an indefinite amount of time by the doctor.

"Perhaps there is someone to help you care for the baby," the doctor suggested.

"I suppose we have no other option," Papa said sadly. "We must do this for the baby's sake." And so, that very night, my mama and papa tucked me into a basket, placed me on the steps of an orphanage, and left town, never to return. Attached to my blanket was a note that read:

PLEASE GIVE ME A HOME.
(AND, IF IT IS NOT TOO MUCH TROUBLE, A NAME.)
                    LOVE,
                    THE BABY

TWO
Pizzazz Shmizazz

Let us leave me and my sad little babiness on the steps of that orphanage for a moment and move across town to the Soap and Suds Car Wash. There worked an elephant. This elephant's name was Birch since he was as white as the bark on a birch tree. Birch worked for a man named the Ringleader. This man had run a circus for fifty years, but when the circus closed, the Ringleader had to run the Soap and Suds Car Wash to make a living. He was pretty bitter about that and treated most of his employees as if they were performers.

"Smile while you wash," he'd tell the boys soaping up the hood of a Chevy. "Arch your back. Point your toes."

He was hardest on Birch. Technically, all Birch's job entailed was sucking up clean water with his trunk out of a wooden barrel, then spraying the soap off the cars. This made Birch sad because an elephant's trunk is an amazing thing. It shouldn't be wasted on washing cars. It should be doing things like touching and lifting. It should be greeting and caressing. It should be doing all the important things.

But the Ringleader didn't care about that, and nothing Birch did was ever good enough for his boss. "Birch, I want to see some pizzazz," the Ringleader would say. "I want to see showmanship. I want to see your zest for the performance."

But Birch had no pizzazz. No showmanship. No zest. In fact, he had never much liked being in the circus, or working at the car wash, or being told what to do at all. Pizzazz shmizazz! Birch felt, as many people do, that he was meant for a life full of more . . . more . . . more something.

And why would an elephant think this? It all started, as many dreams do, with a glimpse of pure beauty.

It was spring and the circus was in Paris for a week. During a break between shows, Birch decided to do a little sightseeing and wandered over to the Louvre, a very impressive museum. He had a hunch they wouldn't let him inside, so he lingered by a side entrance where he saw men moving paintings out of the building and loading them onto a truck. And that's when he *almost* saw it.

The painting was large and rectangular and covered with layers of padding inside a crate. One of the men carrying the painting saw Birch staring at it and stopped. "You like art, big guy?" the man asked the elephant. "This was painted by a man who had a long white beard, same color as you."

Birch's eyes got wide. His heart wondered what the artist had painted.

"It's a painting of a bird that dies in flames and is born again from ashes," the man said. "A phoenix."

Birch never did get to see the painting. But for the rest of his time in the circus, he haunted the tents and cotton-candy stands whispering to the wind about the time he *almost* saw a painting of a phoenix.

In the meantime, the painting sat in the cold basement of an art restoration business, its paint fading and chipping, its colors staring out at the world waiting to be refurbished by an artist to whom it did not belong.

But what a glorious masterpiece Birch imagined all those years. He envisioned the artist walking the wild fields among

scarlet and gold, searching for the right colors to paint the phoenix. The artist painted by dipping his brush into the flowers and used the stream like a child's water glass to wash his tools, turning it milky brown. He worked until the ink-colored night surrounded him. He continued painting without his eyes, knowing that in the morning the dark would be gone. Maybe the blackness became a bird as well—a raven spreading its strong onyx wings and departing at dawn.

The most glorious works of art, the ones that bring the purest joy—perhaps they need not be touched or known, but seen only with the heart.

Birch often thought about the painting while he washed cars at the Soap and Suds. The way the bubbles formed on the hoods of the cars and caught rainbows of color—blue, green, and iridescent pink, like the inside of a clamshell—made him long to be an artist.

"Back to work. Stop daydreaming," the Ringleader yelled, and popped the bubble Birch had been staring at. The dream rose up, humming like a swarm of bees, and departed.

Birch knew that throughout history there have been many jobs that elephants have performed.

Elephant Jobs:

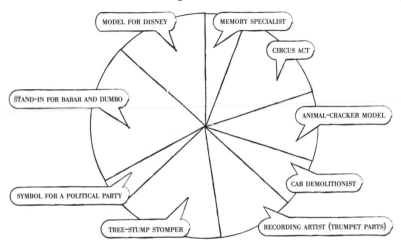

With elephants' vast employment history, it was not inconceivable that one could be an artist. It was, however, unheard of. And, as with most unheard-of things, there must be a first one to do it before it can be spoken on the tongues of history: the first one able to make us stand still long enough to be astonished by the world.

And so life was mostly a dream for Birch until the day a baby—me to be exact—crawled in and lit up his world like a firefly under the bell of a flower.

THREE
As Simple as This

I was born a restless sort, a tumbleweed, a wanderer if you will, and the night my parents left me on the orphanage steps, I didn't wait around to be found. I crawled right out of that basket and made my way into the world.

I crawled clear across town and settled for the night in a pile of leaves near a building housing an old car wash. Around midnight a storm arrived, racing from the edge of the forest, changing quickly from a few fat drops to curtains of water and sideways-blowing wind. Every man, woman, child, cat, and mouse huddled inside and listened to the sound of the water on the tin roofs. There are some people in the world who immediately close the windows when it begins to rain and other people who run outside. As fate would have it, Birch and I both fell into this second group.

Not far away from me stood an ancient tree. On one large limb, it held a dense garden of moss and orchids and other plants that have a hankering to grow up high. The rain filled up the bugle bells made by the curled leaves, as well as saturated the dirt around the roots, and finally the weight became unbearable for the old tree after all those years on earth. First an especially strong gust of wind whipped, and a limb broke and crashed to the ground. Then the tree swayed and creaked, finally slicing through the smaller trees and bushes like the parting of the Red Sea. The tree lay on its side, a portion of the root system exposed, bathed in the deep black soil. When the tree fell, it fell a foot away from where I was sleeping. The bang woke me, but I didn't cry. Birch saw me just the same.

He approached slowly, put his trunk down, and used it to sniff my head. It felt like a suction cup, and I laughed. He lifted me up with his trunk until I was eye-to-eye with him. "My name is Birch," he said. "They call me that because I'm white, like a birch tree."

"Agga blap gurgle," I replied.

"I suppose you'll need a name," Birch said. "And since I'm named after a tree, and you're so tiny, maybe you could be named after a bird. It should be something noble. Something regal. Something elegant. Maybe Falcon or Hawk. Snipe or Kingfisher. Finch or—"

Just then, a clumsy bird landed on the branch of a tree near us. It was fat and gray and had several feathers missing. I liked that bird. I clapped my hands and giggled.

"Pigeon?" Birch said. "You want to be named Pigeon?"

I clapped my hands again.

"But pigeons are disgusting," Birch said. "They're the rats of the bird world. They eat garbage. They're too fat to fly more than five feet."

"Excuse me," the pigeon said to Birch. "But not all of us can be as svelte as you." The pigeon stayed on her branch and sang us a few songs before leaving. She wasn't very good, but I liked the sound. I suppose it reminded me of home.

"Pigeon it is, little baby," Birch said. "And you'll need a last name, something simple, something like Jones. Yes, Jones." And that, friends, is how I became Pigeon Jones.

The next morning Birch approached the Ringleader. The elephant made a trumpeting sound and then held me up for the Ringleader to see.

"That baby has extraordinarily large ears," the Ringleader sneered. "Back in the circus days, I might have been able to give him a job as a big-eared circus freak, but now all I have is this car wash. Do you want me to . . . wash the baby, perhaps?"

Birch shook his head no. He picked up the bucket he used to wash cars and threw it out the door. He lifted a sponge and threw that too, just to make his point.

The Ringleader looked confused. "Quit? You quit? You can barely stop daydreaming long enough to rinse the cars. You're the least talented elephant I've ever met and you quit? You're fired!"

Even as a baby, I didn't like the Ringleader one bit. I didn't

17

like his haughty tone or his curled mustache. I didn't like the way he quickly scuttled from place to place like a crab scrambling sideways over his own shadow.

The first thing Birch did after becoming unemployed was to spend some money. He went to the store and bought a basket. Inside the basket he placed a baby blanket, a rattle, and a bottle of milk. Birch lifted the basket onto his back and then, using his trunk, put me inside. He really did look like a birch tree now, with black wrinkles against white bark and a small nest in his branches.

I looked around with my big baby eyes. The view from Birch's back was nothing but endless blue sky. I saw the shape of a giant bird overhead, circling like a mobile over a crib. For a moment it sailed past the sun, so all I could see was its silhouette. I cooed, and then it flapped, and the world was once again full of lovely, lovely light. I soon fell asleep to the steady drum of Birch's heartbeat saying over and over, *"Thank you. Thank you. Thank you."*

Birch lived near the edge of town and slept in a makeshift house, which was really just a roof with three walls made from planks of wood off old circus train cars. The boards had pictures of animals painted on them, but when Birch took them apart and put them back together, the animal parts got mixed up. Now the walls had lion heads on hippo bodies and monkey feet attached to alligator smiles. That's where Birch and I slept, and we both felt pretty good about that, since nobody could reach me without a ladder.

That first night I found it hard to sleep and tossed and turned on Birch's back. All the commotion woke him up and, as gently as he could, he reached his trunk over his head and inside the basket. Slowly, he tickled my stomach with the tip of his trunk, then pulled away, then tickled again. I smiled, then laughed, and reached out my tiny hands.

A baby's hands are, some would say, the softest things in the world. An elephant's skin is not. An elephant's skin feels like the dry heel on the foot of a man without shoes. However, when I placed my hand on his trunk, Birch knew he had never experienced anything so delicate in his entire life. As he felt my newborn touch, he said, "Where has this been? I've been looking everywhere to feel something as simple as this."

FOUR

The Too-Small-for-a-Name Town

Many people think living on the back of an elephant is pretty strange, but I always felt safe with Birch, like those tiny fish that live harmlessly under the bellies of sharks. Safety, like love, is an odd thing, and it doesn't always come in a package that we get to choose. Because elephants are so fiercely protective of their babies, I was never allowed to leave Birch's back. I mean never, never. Never ever. It's where I slept, ate, played, and showered with the help of Birch's water-loaded trunk. I didn't mind. By the time I was nine years old, I even had my own how-dah house on Birch's back. That was where I kept my few personal effects: my toothbrush, chamber pot, comb, and books. An elephant's back is closer to the sun, and my world was calm, bleached with warmth and brightness.

Plus, there are lots of people who were raised by animals:

People Raised by Animals:

NAME AND AGE	LOCATION	YEAR FOUND	RAISED BY
Andrei, 7	Russia	2004	Dogs
Daniel, 12	Andes, Peru	1990	Goats
Shamdeo, 4	Sultanpur, India	1972	Wolves
Saharan, 15	Syria	1960	Gazelles
Sidi, 15	North Africa	1945	Ostriches
The Turkish Bear-Girl, 9	Turkey	1937	Bears
Assicia, age unknown	Liberia	1930	Monkeys
Leopard Boy of Dihungi, 5	India	1915	Leopards
Skiron, age unknown	Trikkala, Greece	1891	Sheep

Furthermore, the people in my town weren't easy to shock since the place was full of circus performers. A long time ago the circus would settle down during the off-season in a small town. The town was so small that it didn't even have a name. One winter the circus shut down for good, and most of the folks said, "Staying put here is just as fine as staying put somewhere else," and they stayed in the too-small-for-a-name town. Soon it became a normal place full of not-so-normal folks.

There were some former circus performers who fell into their new professions easily after the circus shut down: Franz the Fire-Eater became a well-respected fire chief and Jacques the Giant painted houses. "I don't even need a ladder," he'd explain. Four-Arm Fanny started flipping burgers at the local diner, and there was no stopping her spatula. And there was Finn the Thin Man—he cleaned chimneys, just slipped right up inside.

Since I never had the chance to really know my parents, I made up stories about their lives. I told them to myself so many times before falling asleep, they began to seem close to real, like paintings of memories, like works of art where liberties have been taken with tone and scale. I could look through the broken colors and see their lives. My mama and papa had worked in the traveling circus too. Yes, why, I bet that's how they met. I imagine my mama was the bearded lady, and if I could just talk to her now, she would tell me the story of how she grew her beard. "I was the beautiful daughter of a rich man," Mama would say. "And my father wanted to marry me to a neighboring merchant, but I did not love him and prayed constantly to be spared this fate. The night before the wedding, I grew a beard, which immediately extinguished my future husband's ardor."

And then she met Papa. I bet when he saw her for the first time he thought she was lovely. If I could just talk to him now, he would say things like "If everyone else thinks something is ugly, but you think it's beautiful, then that's a sure symptom of true love."

I imagine that in the circus Papa wore a frog suit and was known as the Frog Swallower, on account of his near-perfect control over his gastrointestinal system. Here's what he would do: He would drink huge amounts of water, then swallow live frogs, salamanders, and even small snakes. Minutes later he would spew them forth, still very much alive and wriggling. Mama probably fell in love with how kind he was to things— inside and out. She knew if he was that gentle in his stomach, he must be even more gentle in his heart.

And so I figured it out: my parents had left me as a

baby so they could run off with a circus, and once again perform as the Frog Swallower and the Bearded Lady. Sometimes
I dreamed that they came back for me, and that I joined the
circus too. I would stand on Birch's back and we would zip
around the center ring. Everyone would cheer and yell, "Look
at that boy! Look how brave!" The only other thing I ever dreamed
was that I could hear my mama crying softly in the next room,
but when I awoke, the only sound was Birch's breathing. Can
you even imagine that? Missing someone so much you would
give anything just to hear her cry again?

FIVE

A Painting Elephant

"Listen," I said to Birch one night as the sky thickened with black-blue darkness. "Can you hear all the animals?" There were sounds of crickets, frogs, and cicadas in the trees. There was a certain rhythm to the song, caused by each creature waiting for a pause to sing. "I can hear things in the pauses too."

"Such as?" Birch asked.

"Oh, well, the moon for example."

"You were listening to the moon? Well, those ears of yours are special, aren't they?"

"Conversing, actually," I replied. "The moon was talking about how he's sick of his literary work, what with all his appearances in stories. Tired of being full of cheese and drawing werewolves near. But then I asked him, 'What would you do if we didn't need you? If we told you we were fine with just our lamps and light-up gear?' The moon agreed he'd miss his career."

We sat there in the quiet. The mosquitoes nibbled on my skin, reminding me where the world ends and I begin. "Know what else I asked the moon?" I said to Birch. "I asked him if maybe, while he's already up there in the sky, he can find my family, if they're still alive."

"Well, that seems like a reasonable enough request," Birch replied.

"Do you think Mama and Papa remember me?" I asked.

"I know they do," Birch said. "I know because I loved someone and lost someone once too," he continued. "Love is like rain. I remember how it fell down on my back, the water spraying off me like the sparks of a firecracker. I felt every raindrop. I felt the oceans where they had been, the clouds they flew from, and the adventures they had in front of them—adventures on petals of flowers, on wings of bees, or in the dark soil. In the rain, I was flawless and wild with the skies falling over me like gray and blue silk. I didn't ever want to come in out of that rain."

My heart hurt. Of course, I didn't need to say this to Birch for him to know what I was thinking. After so many years of constant togetherness, my eyes were Birch's, and his mine. Trunk and nose were interchangeable, and we breathed the same breath. Even our movements came together like a flock of geese changing direction, first in our minds, then in the air. So, without a word being spoken, Birch always knew when I was upset. He'd reach his trunk over his head, wrap it around me, and stay like that until I drifted off to sleep.

After tucking me in, Birch would quietly get out the art kit he'd bought at a secondhand store. He'd set up his easel and lay his tubes of oil paint out in specific rainbow order: red, orange, yellow, green, blue, indigo, and violet. He'd squeeze some of the blue on a palette and then, gripping a paintbrush in his trunk, cover the soft bristles with deep color. Then he'd take a breath, whispering, "This is my favorite part," and make the first stroke on a pure white canvas.

Since Birch was an animal and part of nature, he created art the way nature creates it. Nature's art is the spider's web or the nest of a bird with twigs layered with precision, tied together with a strand of a girl's silky hair; a silkworm's cocoon, spun like sugar, a cotton-candy delicacy; the tapping of a light-drunk moth against a screen door. It's the leaves of fall stained scarlet and, in turn, their reflection rendering a lake scarlet as well; a school of silver fish darting together or the way a savannah of grass and a herd of bison and a blue sky can create stripes of color on a horizon.

That night Birch painted a picture of a late summer evening using all the colors on his palette. He painted an orange sky pouring buckets of light onto a field that stretched back to a black fringe of forest. He painted a river reflecting the sky, a river that was silent and always moving toward the ocean, toward a place where we could rediscover long-lost love. He painted birds in a tree by the riverbank, and imagined they were speaking to the river and singing to the grasses. If the song was truly beautiful, Birch imagined that everything was singing together with those birds—the dirt, the mountains, and the leaves—and the dreams of things that can't sing could be heard in the things that can.

SIX

Scientific Names and Other Zoological Facts

"Well, you have to start the fifth grade tomorrow, Pigeon," Birch said one day, as if I needed a haircut or new underpants.

"You're joking, right?" I replied.

"Not at all," Birch said. "Homeschooling is over. I've taught you what I know."

The night before I was to start school, lying on Birch's back, I decided to count the stars. But the stars wouldn't come out to be counted, so I decided to count the holes they left. I remembered the time I had seen a shooting star, and for some reason it made my heart feel sad. Lots of people think they're beautiful, but I thought about how the star had lived in the sky, and now it was forced to leave the world it had known for somewhere else. A falling star must have far to fall, and probably a lot of bumps, bruises, and scars when it's all said and done.

The next morning Birch handed me freshly pressed pants and a new collared shirt and I got dressed standing on his back. Birch used his trunk to comb my hair over to the side.

"I look like a fool," I told him.

"You look like a gentleman," Birch said, adjusting the large striped tie he'd placed around his own neck. "I want us both to look presentable. You only get one chance to make a first impression."

"The impression we're making is that we dress like total fools," I replied.

Soon the minibus pulled up. There were already about five children inside, and the driver just stared at us with her face scrunched up tight like she was trying to do long division in her head.

"My name is Pigeon Jones," I said. "I

live on the back of this elephant named Birch. Today is my first day of fifth grade."

The driver stared with her mouth agape. "That elephant you're riding won't fit on this bus, boy," she said, wiping her brow with a handkerchief.

"He isn't going to fit in a classroom neither," said a thin boy with no front teeth. His two friends laughed and held their hands up to their ears. "You look like an elephant too with those big ears," one said.

"I suppose," the driver said, "you and your elephant—"

"Birch. His name is Birch," I interrupted.

"All right, I suppose you and Birch can walk along beside the bus until we get to school. That way you won't get lost." And that's just what we did. As we walked along, I noticed I was riding next to a window. Through it I could see a girl in a polka-dot dress reading a book and stealing glances at Birch.

"Don't you get motion sickness if you read while someone is driving?" I asked her. "I sure do."

She stared in my direction. "When are you ever in a car if you live on the back of an *Elephas maximus indicus*?"

"Well, that's what I meant. I can only read if Birch isn't

walking." I scratched my head. "Hey, what did you call Birch? An Ela-maxa-whata?"

"*Elephas maximus indicus.* It's his scientific name." She held up the book she was reading, and it had the title *Scientific Names and Other Zoological Facts* on the front.

"I want to be a zoologist," she said.

"What does a zoologist do, exactly?" I asked. She had a lonesome look about her, but her eyes glittered just a little when she started to answer.

"Oh, being a zoologist is the best job there is. You get to be around animals all day long. Wild animals like zebras and lions. Animals that you wouldn't normally get to go near, but they let you, because you're a zoologist and wild animals know to trust zoologists. That's just part of their instincts."

"Wow, you sure are smart. Maybe I'd like to be a zoologist," I said.

"You can't be a zoologist from the back of an elephant," the girl replied. "Unless you came down, of course."

"Oh, I never leave Birch's back. I don't know why I ever would. So," I continued, "if you want to be a zoologist, you must be thrilled to see a real elephant." I patted Birch and flashed her a winning smile.

She blushed as red as the polka dots on her dress. "Maybe a tad excited," she said. "Everyone calls me Darling, by the way. Darling Clementine, if you were wondering."

"Of course," I said, speaking quickly. "What a swell name. Boy-oh-boy. This town is so magical, don't you think? I never noticed before."

She rolled her eyes and was so cute, it felt like someone had reached inside me and pulled my stomach inside out like a sock.

I, Pigeon Jones, had fallen in love.

SEVEN
The Elephant (Not Quite) in the Room

My teacher seemed nice enough, except he spat whenever he said the letter P. As luck would have it, my classroom was on the first floor. This was lucky because it allowed Birch to stand outside the open window, and I was able to stay on his back but still see and hear the teacher. It also helped me avoid being spat upon every time the teacher said "Pigeon." However, I seemed to be the only one following along with the lesson. None of the students were interested in Mr. Turnipseed's lecture on Shakespeare—they all seemed more interested in the big white elephant in the room. Well, not in the room. The big white elephant right *outside* the room.

"Mr. Turnipseed," a young boy in overalls said without raising his hand. "Were there any elephants in Shakespeare's plays?" The students laughed. "Maybe Juliet talked to Romeo from the back of an elephant instead of a balcony!"

"Mr. Turnipseed, can you speak up a bit?" a second boy asked. "I can't hear you with my normal-sized ears."

"Mr. Turnipseed." A girl with very thick glasses raised her hand. "Do elephants bite? They have such big, scary teeth." The class erupted into laughter. Darling Clementine turned around and gave me a look of what could only be described as pity.

"Children, please purify the things you're pondering. I am preaching about Shakespeare here, about proud Romeo and purest Juliet, the most passionate of passionate productions. I don't want to hear another peep," Mr. Turnipseed said, turning back to his lesson. The unfortunate boy in the seat closest to the board took off his glasses and cleaned away the spittle on them with his shirtsleeve.

"Those are not teeth."

Mr. Turnipseed whirled back around. "Who pronounced that peep?" he bellowed.

"They're tusks," replied Darling Clementine. "Not teeth."

"That's it, young lady!" Mr. Turnipseed said, pointing. "That was a peep! Preposterous, pointed peeping. You have officially lost your lunchtime privileges."

When lunchtime came, I sat on Birch's back and watched the other boys play baseball in the field next to the school. I wanted to play, but there's no position for a boy who always stays on the back of an elephant. All I wanted to think about, to be honest, was Darling Clementine and how she had defended

Birch to the other students. I decided this quality was one I liked in a woman.

"Birch," I said, "go over to that water fountain." We marched over to the drinking fountain and Birch sucked up a trunk full of water. "Now go stand next to Mr. Turnipseed's classroom and let's make it rain."

And that's just what we did. Standing beside the classroom window, Birch sprayed water up in the air.

"Oh dear," Mr. Turnipseed shouted. "It's raining! I need to pop out and roll up my car windows before my perfect leather interior is poured upon." He looked at Darling sitting in detention. "You better proceed out to recess where the chaperone on duty can properly pay attention to you."

"Yes, sir," said Darling with a smile.

Once she got outside, Darling ran up to thank us, but the water coming from Birch's trunk poured down on her. "Oh no! You got my dress all rained on," she yelled.

There's music in a girl's hair, in the shaking out of water. There are wind chimes in it, tiny, tinkling echoes of the sound you can hear carried by a breeze sometimes. Droplets leaped from her hair, shimmering; one landed on my lip. Without taking my eyes off her, I licked it away, and it tasted like heaven. Darling pretended to be disgusted about being wet, disgusted by the recklessness of water, the way that girls sometimes do. But no matter how hard she was working not to smile, I saw a twinkle in her eyes and knew she had secretly enjoyed it. Oh, who knew a girl's hair could have so much to say, or even tongue to say it?

EIGHT

Red Balloons

"Birch. Birch, are you awake?" I asked that night when I was supposed to be asleep.

"I am now," he replied.

"Birch, tell me about the time you were in love," I said, thinking of the droplet of water from Darling's hair that had landed on my lip.

We sat there for a moment listening to the crickets crick.

"I fell in love with an acrobat when I worked for the circus," Birch said. "She joined a few years after I did. Her name was Dahlia, like the flower, like the color red. We performed an act together where she would do flips and handstands on my back. She was so beautiful. She would wear outfits in bright orange and red with sparkles all over them and feathers in her hair. She looked like a great flaming phoenix rising from the ashes on my back as I trotted around the ring."

"Did she love you too?"

"It's hard to say," Birch replied. "It's hard to say with love. But I do remember once she came by to say good night and she gave me a bag of peanuts. And do you know what she said? She said, 'I brought you these because I like seeing you happy.' It was the most romantic moment of my entire life."

I thought about the girl on Birch's back, her hands planted on his shoulders, her legs in the air together, then split apart, her toes pointed like a ballerina's. It must have been hard to keep her balance. She must have really trusted Birch.

"Then one day they added a new trick to our act," Birch whispered. "She would stand on my back, and I'd pick up speed and then WHOOSH! Another acrobat would sweep down from the sky on a swing and lift her off my back. They'd do their tumbling routine with me standing below watching. It was a very popular act, but I hated it."

"Why?"

"Every time she was lifted away, it felt like a part of me was being taken. I'd look up and she would get smaller and smaller

41

like a red balloon, its string accidentally let loose from a child's hand, floating higher and higher."

I laid my head on Birch's shoulders and let my body rise and fall with his breath. "That's the thing," Birch said, "about balloons. Airy and light, but don't attach anything to one that you ever want to see again." Birch wiped a tear from his eye with his trunk. "Never get attached to someone, Pigeon. You'll spend the rest of your days waiting for that person to come back, or worse, waiting for *yourself* to come back. Never get attached to beauty. Never get attached to your own beauty. To pictures of beauty. The cities you saw will never be the same; the streets will grow old as well, the neighbors turning gray in their houses. Don't get attached to hope. I tell you there's no ship coming. I tell you there's no road away from this place where we stand."

We sat together, and finally I asked, "You don't really believe any of that, do you?" In reply, Birch reached over and lifted the cloth that covered his canvases. As he turned several of them around, I saw that they were all paintings of a great orange and red bird of paradise, a beautiful creature, painted with tiny bristled brushes and so detailed the feathers looked real. I imagined if I put my palms flat against those birds, I would feel heat radiating from their bodies.

"She fell in love with the other acrobat," Birch said. "They ran off together to Paris and I've never seen her since. I guess that's not true, because I see her everywhere. When I see goldenrod dancing in the wind in summertime, or when I see a firefly blink on and off like a lighthouse over the ocean, or when I see moonlight streaking the wing of a bird."

"Where do they go, Birch?"

"Where does what go, Pigeon?" Birch said, sounding sleepy.

"All those *feelings* that you had for her. I mean, they came out of you, and then they went out into the world. What happened to them? They can't just disappear."

"I suppose not," Birch said, yawning, his trunk whistling

like a distant train. "Perhaps they travel the world forever. Spiraling, twirling, dancing through the wet grass. Perhaps, if we're lucky, we will happen upon them again when we least expect it." Then Birch fell asleep, dreaming he had wings to fly—fly up high and catch all the world's red balloons.

NINE

The Amazing
Singing Hoboes

And so the next few months passed in much the same way: I'd get made fun of at school, avoid being spat on by Mr. Turnipseed, and secretly pine for the love of Darling Clementine. The only thing that cheered me up was the approach of my tenth birthday.

"What would you like?" Birch asked. "You can have anything at all."

"Anything?"

Birch made the mistake of once again saying, "Yes, anything."

"Okay, then I want to go to the train station."

"Your birthday wish is a train? That may be a bit extravagant."

"No, it's only the first part of what I'd like. Just last night, when I couldn't sleep, I realized what we had to do. Why, it was as if I had been gazing at a twig and then suddenly realized what I was really looking at was a cleverly disguised insect."

"I'm afraid you've lost me," replied Birch.

"You said the lady acrobat left you to go to Paris. And Paris is where all the famous artists go and hang out. Isn't it obvious? We need to go to Paris! We need to go and find your love and make you the famous artist you've always dreamed of being."

"What about school?"

"School vacation. It's perfect!" Birch hesitated and I crossed my arms. "You said *anything*."

"So that's really your birthday wish? Paris?"

I smiled, knowing I had won.

The next day Birch and I found a freight train heading to New York—a city where there are lots of planes traveling to Paris. The train stopped, and as I said to Birch, "I'm not sure you're going to fit," a voice on the train said the same exact words. It was an old man, a hobo, without any teeth. "You can try, though," he went on to say. "I've never been one to discriminate against bigger-boned folks."

Birch nodded and climbed through the freight car door. He had to crouch down and kneel once inside so my head didn't hit the ceiling, but overall, it was a pretty successful maneuver. The train rumbled through towns that had names I didn't know, and when we shot into a tunnel through the mountain, the lights flickered once, then twice, and then went out. During those few moments of darkness, I imagined I was an astronaut on a ship zipping through space and, if I looked out the window and behind us, I'd see the earth—every person I'd ever known and every place I'd ever been. Every tree, every moon, and every voice. All the sadness, and the loneliness and the happiness too, all reduced to a speck so small that if I closed one eye and held up my thumb, I could block it all out. My entire world. Gone. Just like that.

"Don't be scared, youngster," the toothless old man said as the lights flickered back on. "Train does that sometimes, loses its will to go on, I suppose. Always gets it back soon enough, though, just like the rest of us."

"I'm Pigeon," I replied. "And this is Birch."

"Well, those are mighty fine names indeed," the man said. "My name is Pocketless Pete, on account of my pants ain't got no pockets. And these are my friends."

Three more hoboes stepped out of the shadows and smiled. "I'm Hatshoe Harry," the first man said. He was wearing a porkpie hat in place of his left shoe.

"I'm Kittenbeard Kip," the second man said. Something meowed suspiciously from his knee-length beard.

"And I'm Beancan Bill," the third man said. "And this is my singing bean can." He held an empty aluminum can in his hand like a puppet. The lid was still attached and did, in fact, look like a mouth.

"We're a singing group," Pocketless Pete said. "We're called the Amazing Singing Hoboes. Would you like to hear a song?"

"Well, that would be wonderful, sir," I said.

The four hoboes cleared their throats, and Beancan Bill blew into a harmonica to get things started. "Let's sing 'em the blues, boys."

Hobo Blues

You know I | dream about pants with some pockets | When I hear that empty train whistle call

Yes I | dream about pants with some pockets | When I hear that empty train whistle call | 'Cause the

only thing sadder than empty pockets | Is having no pockets at—all

"So," I asked, "are all your songs about not having pockets?"

"I suppose they are," Pete said. "They say to write what you know, and I know what it's like not to have pockets." He sat next to the window and a ray of sun found his cheek, illuminating a scar that ran down the side of his face like twine. I wondered where it was from, but I didn't ask. I guess there are some sorrows in the world even a choir of angels couldn't unravel with a song.

"Could I ask you a question, young man?" Pete asked.

"Sure."

"Are you going to finish that ham sandwich?"

I had half a sandwich that we'd bought on the road left over, the edge of which was hanging out of my pocket. "Probably," I said. "I'm saving it for later."

"That's the right thing to do," Pete said, smiling. "On the road, you never know where your next meal will come from. It's time for our afternoon nap, but remember, when the train drops you off, take the subway into the Bronx."

"But we're headed to the airport," I said.

"Make a stop before you get there," he said. "There's something in the Bronx that I'm sure you two would enjoy. And remember," he added, "never forget how to sing, Pigeon. Never ever."

While they were asleep, I helped Birch leave them a special surprise. Birch got out his paints and brushes and went to work on the walls of that old train car. He painted a stage with velvet curtains and a neon sign that read BLUES JOINT. He painted an audience seated at tables, smiling and clapping. And, last but not least and with special care, he painted a set of pockets on the worn cloth of Pocketless Pete's pants.

Birch and I had to get off the train before they awoke, so we didn't see their reaction, but I like to think they were pleased. I like to think that when Pete woke up, he was excited to see his imaginary pockets and also to see the ham sandwich I'd left him.

"Why, I have pockets!" he'd exclaim. "And look, inside there's a sandwich." I like to think he'd take a giant bite of ham and cheese and mustard, then close his eyes like he had heaven in his mouth. Then he'd take a few slices of ham out of the sandwich and feed them to a dog with a dirty bandanna around his neck. The dog would smile the same way the old man did, and the two of them would sit together in the open door of the train car, their hearts glowing just as bright as the sunset.

TEN

The Great Golden God

After we left the train, we followed Pocketless Pete's advice and made our way to the subway. Birch, however, did not fit through the turnstile.

"Excuse me," I said to the man in the subway booth. "Do you happen to know of a place in the Bronx that would be of interest to a boy and an elephant?"

"Well, the Bronx Zoo isn't too far. Maybe you'd like it there."

And so we set out. However, after a few blocks, it became clear that we were obstructing the flow of traffic. Cars stopped and drivers craned their necks out windows to see Birch. A police officer approached, speaking frantically into his radio. Birch, intrigued by all the colors of the city, didn't seem worried. "Why, Pigeon, what a lovely uniform that officer is wearing," he said. "What color do you think it is? Royal? Cobalt? Midnight blue?"

"Don't panic, little boy!" The officer blew his whistle and continued shouting. "I've called for a truck to take that elephant to the zoo."

"How wonderful," I replied. "That's exactly where we're headed."

The officer looked confused. Unsure what to do, he blew his whistle once again. A few minutes later, a flatbed truck arrived and Birch and I were on our way. "What a nice, helpful officer," Birch said. "And his uniform was definitely forget-me-not blue."

The truck pulled up to the back entrance at the zoo. Before Birch and I knew what was happening, several zoo workers had approached and were circling around us with giant nets and snare poles. "Don't worry, little boy," one said to me, "we'll save you."

"I don't need to be saved," I replied.

"He's delirious with fear," another zookeeper said.

"I'm not delirious with fear," I told him. "We just wanted to visit the zoo."

Of course they didn't believe us, because an elephant near the zoo is automatically considered an escapee, as we learned that day. And that, my friends, is how Birch and I were locked up within the first twenty-four hours of our great adventure.

When the guards tried to take me down off Birch's back, I threw a fit, kicking my legs, hollering, and attempting to bite a guard's hand, so they left me where I was for the time being. We were placed in a holding pen and could hear some of the other animals milling about: the lions yawning, the birds squawking, and the monkeys throwing things at one another. The day turned to deepest night, and we were still confused as to what our fate would be.

"Hello?" I said. "Can anyone hear me? We're not supposed to be in this zoo."

"As if anyone is supposed to be here," a bored voice said with a French accent. "I'm from France. Do you even know where that is?"

"Who said that?"

"I did," the voice said. "*Bonjour.* I'm a turtle and they call me Pierre."

"Pierre, we're trapped here," I told him.

"It may seem to you that you are trapped in that small pen," the turtle said from over the wall, "but truthfully you've been able to leave the whole time. There's a door behind you, hidden in the shadows." I looked behind us, and squinted to see in the dark. Birch felt around with his trunk. Slowly, slowly, something started to move. There was, in fact, a door. And so we opened it and stepped on through.

"Birch, look. It's so beautiful."

All around us was a lush, verdant paradise. There were trees of every size and a watering hole where several animals stood, dipping their heads into the placid water. A giraffe and her calf ate from a tree, and busy birds chatted noisily. Nobody seemed to notice us.

"Not exactly freedom," Pierre said. "But more in accordance with our rights than solitary confinement." Birch and I made our way to a small patch of flowers, and Birch lay down for a rest. When he lowered himself to the ground, a great cloud of yellow pollen from all the flowers rose up around us like a thick fog, and then settled down again. Birch and I sat there, watching the sunrise over the walls of the zoo. The light crept slowly, first illuminating the farthest corner of the enclosure, and then stretching across the field like it was unfurling a roll of wrapping paper. When the light finally hit us, we heard a great chatter go up from around the watering hole. A crowd started to form around us, so we stood up to greet them.

"Gadzooks!" a gazelle shouted. "The Great Golden God has come!"

"It's him," said a cockatoo.

"We're not worthy," a zebra said, leaning forward, head bowed.

"I'm sorry, are you speaking to us?" I asked.

"Of course," the gazelle replied. "We have been waiting for you for so long. You are here to free us. The Golden God we knew would come." He pointed his hoof toward the watering hole. In the center of the small pond sat a water fountain in the shape of a great, golden elephant god. And on the golden elephant's back sat a boy just about my age. As the sun hit us, each ray reflected off the million specks of golden pollen covering Birch's skin and made us a mirror image to the statue.

"You've come to free us," a monkey said. "That is what the

legend says. That's what my father told me, and his father told
him."

"If you'll excuse us, we need to have a word in private," I
said. The animals nodded solemnly and backed away.

"Birch," I said, and then sneezed because of the pollen up my nose. "Birch, this could be our chance to get out of here. We have an entire zoo full of animals rallied around us, ready to do whatever we tell them."

"I agree," Birch said. "I just hope it doesn't rain and wash away all my great golden power."

ELEVEN
Svelte Hippos and Colorful Zebras

I stood on Birch's back in front of the other animals with my chest puffed out, like a sailor standing on the prow of a ship. Our golden hue gave off an intense shine, and the sun was hot. We were light within light, like a match flame struck on the brightest of days. "We have a plan," I shouted to the animals.

"They have a plan!" the monkeys shouted back.

"A plan to free us all," I continued.

"A plan to free us all!" the monkeys shouted.

"Monkeys, please."

"Sorry," they replied, blushing.

"This plan," I continued, "was inspired by a legend I once read." The animals all nodded. They were pleased. Animals like legends.

"I read that the Hindus believe that the world rests upon an elephant. And the elephant rests upon the back of a giant turtle. But what, you may ask, does the turtle rest upon? The Hindus would tell you, 'Something, but we know not what.'"

"Huh?" the monkeys said, scratching their heads.

"What I'm saying is that we will build on this idea of animals resting upon animals, supporting the world. We'll stand on one another's backs, and rise higher and higher until one of us can climb over the wall and unlock the gate."

"Brilliant!" they all shouted. "Magnificent!"

"We have to wait until nightfall," I said. "In the meantime, everyone go roll around in the golden pollen and prepare for freedom."

And so we waited. Soon the zoo closed for the day, and the sun set at a languid pace. To pass the time until dark, Birch took out his easel and paints and did portraits of the different animals.

"I'd like to look svelte," a hippopotamus told Birch as he painted her. Of course, she didn't need to say anything; Birch had a special knack for painting his subjects exactly how they wished to look, as if he took their deepest desire, laid it out on his palette, and then dipped his brush into their dreams. The slim hippo, the colorful zebra, the nimble sloth: they all saw the paintings and exclaimed, "It's me! Yes, that's exactly how I see myself in my heart."

Dusk fell after the hot day and dark heat hugged the walls of the zoo. The animals slipped out of their cages and into the open area by the pond. They had done as we'd asked and each one glowed, covered from head to tail in golden pollen. Marching single file toward the wall of the zoo, they looked like a great processional of glorious statues.

"Elephants and hippos, you'll form our base," I directed. "The next lightest animals—mostly zebras and gazelles—climb on after that. Monkeys and large rodents follow them, and so on, until we reach the top."

We began to pile high when the sound of a door opening and closing was heard in the distance, and footsteps started moving closer and closer. "Don't move a muscle," I whispered, and the animals all held their breath. Two zoo security guards came out into the clearing, their flashlight beams swinging around in front of them like shafts from a lighthouse.

"You see anything suspicious?" one guard asked the other.

"Nothing at all. Just a giant golden totem pole over by that wall."

"Oh, right, that," the second guard replied.

"You have to wonder what they're going to think of next." They shrugged their shoulders, turned, and walked back to the office.

"You two are the most brilliant creatures I've ever met," a monkey told us. "You had us cover ourselves in pollen to fool the dim-witted guards. We'll follow the two of you to the ends of the earth," he continued. The other animals voiced their agreement.

"Well, to be honest," I said, "we're just headed to Paris so Birch can fall in love and be famous."

"You don't go to Paris to become famous," a lizard shouted from the top of the totem. "You go to Hollywood. That's where all the agents are. Once you get an agent, he'll make you famous and *then* you can go hang out with all the artists in Paris."

"Makes sense, I suppose . . ." I replied.

"Hey!" a hippo's voice said loudly from the bottom of the

pile. "Could we perhaps chat about this later, maybe at a time when I'm not carrying a dozen of you idiots on my back?"

"But we need an extra boost," I said. "We're just a tiny ways from the top. Is there anyone else? Anyone?" But everyone was already stretching as far as they could stretch.

"Oh no," an aardvark said, sniffing the air.

"Uh-oh," a porcupine said, quivering her quills.

"What?" I said, hearing nothing.

When a storm is brewing, humans must rely on technology to detect it. Or they just stand and watch the lightning and hear the noise. But the animals know before that. A horse can perk her ears and the birds fly to taller trees. The animals sense a storm is coming before the first cloud, before the first streetlamp bangs against a post in the wind, before the first hoofprint in the sand blows away.

And they were right. A storm was coming fast, and the tops of trees started to shiver. Several animals got scared and started to move around, causing the tower to sway and lean precariously.

"Hurry," I said. "We need to hurry."

Then, suddenly, there was a lurch, and the animals rose up the tiny bit more they needed to rise, and a monkey was able to scramble over the wall. He ran around and unlocked the door, and all the animals climbed down the totem and out the door into the city streets.

"How did that happen?" I asked.

"It was Pierre the turtle," the animals shouted.

"But how? That's impossible," I said. Yet there sat Pierre, a bored expression on his face.

"What wretchedness it must be," he said, "to believe only in what can be proven. We once lived in the sea, *non*? And the moon was once touchable from the earth." We all looked toward the night sky and nodded at the turtle's cosmic explanation.

"Also, I've been working out," Pierre added.

And so we all walked. The storm had passed, we were free, and I couldn't imagine anything in our way. I thought about the earth and how we perceive there to be light and dark. But really, there is only constant light, and it is the earth that spins away into shadow and then toward the brilliance once again.

TWELVE
Catching Silver Fish

"How does it feel to be free?" I asked the animals.

"Good," a monkey said. "I mean, I think it's good. It's an awfully big world out here, isn't it?"

"Yes, but that's one of the best parts about it," I said. "Now let's get onto a plane and fly to Hollywood."

So the collection of golden creatures marched on through the night, crossed over a bridge, and passed through the shadows to Kennedy Airport. There, I wrote out luggage and handle-with-care tags and had all the animals attach them to their limbs. "Now," I told the animals, "remain as still as statues." It worked too; when the baggage handlers came to load the plane, they complained about the passenger who was bringing all these heavy golden statues back to Hollywood.

"Be extra careful," one handler said. "These look expensive."

"Only some movie-star type would buy these. Look at the golden monkeys. Talk about ugly."

Before I could stop him, one of the monkeys stretched out a paw and gave a karate chop to the back of the baggage handler's leg. The man spun around frantically, but the monkey was once again as still as a statue.

"I think I'm losing my marbles," the shaken handler said to his coworker. "Let's get this over with," he added. "I feel like I'm in a zoo."

The plane landed in Los Angeles, and we were unloaded and left on the tarmac for pickup. When the workers went on their lunch break, we just sneaked away and then, like mystical creatures, slipped soundlessly into the shadows.

Birch and I bade farewell to the other animals and wished them luck in their new life of freedom and sunshine. I was unsure what would become of them, but felt hopeful and calm. Birch always taught me that animals have instincts, that they have skies and stars memorized, lit up like wee planetariums behind their wild eyes.

Hollywood was a lot different from where Birch and I came from. The buildings were fancier and the cars were shinier. We visited the Walk of Fame and gazed up at the big H-O-L-L-Y-W-O-O-D letters in the hills. "Look," we heard a woman say, "an elephant! They must be shooting a movie here!" A group of tourists gathered around and snapped pictures. We then went down to the beach, where there was a boardwalk, a Ferris wheel, and big crowds of people. The air smelled like sand, hot asphalt, and something sweet. We bought hot dogs and watched a man strum a lovely song while tourists tossed change into an open ukulele case.

That's when I saw them—a couple standing on the board-walk. They were sharing an apple, the woman taking one bite, then the man, until it was gone. They threw the core in the trash and began dancing to the ukulele song.

"Birch! It's my parents!" I shouted.

"But you haven't seen them since you were a baby. How do you know?"

"I just do. A bearded woman and a man in a frog suit."

We approached them, and when we were behind the couple, Birch tapped them on the shoulder with his trunk.

"Excuse us," I said. The couple turned around, and I realized I'd been mistaken. The bearded woman turned out to be a man with a beard, and the frog turned out to be a woman wearing a green tracksuit and a baseball cap.

"Sorry," I mumbled as we walked away. Trying to find two

people out of the billions on the earth was like trying to catch those tiny silver fish that dart through shallow water in the spring. There are so many, you'd think you could just put your hand in the water and catch some, but that's not the case. Those slivers of silver keep slipping through your fingers time and time again.

Birch treated me to an ice cream cone. We gazed out the big windows of the sweet shop and watched the sun finish its setting. I lifted the body of a dead bee from above a light fixture near the ceiling, and it was almost weightless, this thorax and the crystal wings. How long had it been there? Forever? Sunsets, ukuleles, insects, people, love. The workings of the world were still a mystery to me—a tiny flea circus, wonderful to watch, but with the nuts and bolts still hidden.

THIRTEEN
Slim Spatucci: Talent Guru

I did some research and scheduled a meeting for us with a talent agent so Birch could be discovered. I was surprised when we were escorted into the office with the words SLIM SPATUCCI: TALENT GURU written on the door. When I saw Slim, I noted that his name could have been Squat Spatucci. Or Sunburn Spatucci. Or Silly Toupee Spatucci. Anything but Slim.

"What artistic schooling do you have?" Slim asked Birch without looking up from his paperwork.

"Well, he was a circus performer for a while," I replied.

"Not exactly applicable. Let's see your portfolio." Birch pulled out some of his paintings and showed them to Slim. Slim looked through them excitedly. "Hey, these aren't half bad.

These aren't even a quarter or an eighth bad. I can sell these, no problem."

I could feel Birch's excitement mounting. "Just one thing," Slim said. "Nobody's ever going to believe that a big, silly elephant painted these. So we're gonna tell everyone that you did," he said, pointing at me.

"Me?"

"Yes, *you.* We'll play up the child-genius angle. The press will love it."

"I don't mind," Birch whispered to me. "As long as people get to see my art."

I protested. I listed for Slim Spatucci all the animals I could think of that were also artists. Dogs, cats, and even termites.

TITLE: *La Joie au Muck*, exhibition catalog, Lyon, 1988.
GENRE: Abstract Expressionism; Dogs
DESCRIPTION: The dogs would go outside, play in the mud, and then prance over the light-toned carpets in the house.

TITLE: *La Muse*, temporary installation, dining room carpet, 12×13 cm.
GENRE: Installation Art; Cats
DESCRIPTION: Meticulous construction with hairballs and tangles of yarn on carpet shows great maturity and a clear sense of purpose.

TITLE: *Breakfast*, private collection, wood, 1987.

GENRE: Spontaneous Reductionism; Termites

DESCRIPTION: Termites chew away the wood of a house to reveal large areas of negative space—suggests motifs of greed and destruction.

"Listen, kid," Slim said. "I'm single, I don't dress very well, and I often exude a strange odor. Basically, I don't know much. But I do know art, and nobody's going to buy a painting by an elephant. If anybody asks, *you* did them. End of story."

Little did we know that at the moment Birch and I were signing our lives over to Slim Spatucci, news of our other adventures were filtering back to our too-small-for-a-name town and the evil Ringleader. He sat wearing a monocle over one eye, hunched over the newspaper.

"It says," he read, "that a boy on the back of an elephant spent the night in a zoo and painted the entire inside of the cell. And look there," the Ringleader exclaimed. "There's a photo. That's Birch and his boy, all right."

The article described the paintings, and there were pictures. That night, in the zoo cage, Birch had laid out his paints, palette, and brushes. Looking them over, he decided he'd need mostly blues and greens for the night's project. On the walls he painted a vast forest with thick stretches of trees, ominous shadows, and the glowing eyes of creatures in the night. He filled in the sky above them, and the clouds were so real, it looked like it could rain right there in that dingy, dark zoo cell. Birch stood back and admired his work with pride. It filled his heart with happiness to take a place so ugly and make it so beautiful.

"Rocks are just rocks," he'd said, "until the day someone imagines them as a palace."

The Ringleader got very angry to see how beautiful the paintings were. He liked them about as much as he liked song melodies and kitten paws and ballroom dancing. That is to say, he didn't like them at all.

"'The elephant and boy are no longer in the zoo's custody,'" the Ringleader continued reading. "'However, there has been great interest in Pigeon Jones's paintings from art collectors in New York, London, Paris, and beyond.'

"Well, I'll be," the Ringleader said, putting down the paper. "I know very well that the elephant did those paintings. He was always fiddling with his silly art. A big dumb elephant. A big dumb elephant that's going to make a fortune. A big dumb elephant that belongs to *me*."

FOURTEEN

A Signature Is Not Hard to Find

And soon I, Pigeon Jones, a simple boy, became the most famous artist in America. (Though, technically speaking, I couldn't even draw a stick figure.) I did interviews on the radio, in magazines, and even on a few late-night talk shows.

"So you're a child and an artist," one host said, "and you live on the back of this Indian elephant?"

"Yes, that is correct," I said, and the studio audience clapped.

"You are certainly a unique boy," the host said. "Where *did* you come from?"

"My mother was the Bearded Lady," I replied. "And my father wore a frog suit."

The host scratched his head, and then laughed. "Well,

you're an artist. I suppose you're expected to be a bit . . . eccentric."

You'd think Birch would have been upset that I was getting all the attention for his work, but the truth was, he didn't seem to care at all. At first it confused me, but then one day a very old woman came into the gallery and walked around the room to look at all the paintings. She stopped in front of a painting of a red-dahlia-colored bird and stood there for a long time.

"Are you an artist?" I asked.

"Oh no, not me," she replied. "But my late husband was."

"What did he paint?"

"Well," the woman said, "he painted pictures of me mostly."

Birch closed his eyes and nodded his head, understanding what this meant and that this woman had been loved.

"It was amazing," she continued. "When he painted a picture of me, critics said you could see so much. That you could see every woman any great artist ever painted: Velázquez's sleeper seen in a mirror, Tiepolo's nymph in dewy skies, Boucher's beautiful shepherdess, Fragonard's woman of nobility, Delacroix's golden sultana, Cézanne's bather, Renoir's young woman blissful beneath an endless sun."

The old woman dabbed her eyes with a handkerchief. "The first night I met him, we were standing on the sidewalk waiting for a bus, and he showed me a snapshot of the sky that he kept in his wallet. He said, 'One day, I was lying on the beach in France, and I signed my name on the back of the sky. Ever since that time, I've always hated birds, for they keep trying to make holes in my biggest and most beautiful work.'" She paused, then finally said, "And now, sometimes when the house gets too lonely, I go outside and look up. You know, I think he was wrong about the sky being his finest work of art. I think the life we spent together, though not as lofty, was much greater. I turn my heart over and over and his signature is not hard to find."

I realized then that this is what Birch was doing as well. He was painting the world he loved, a gorgeous world, a place the size of heaven. A world you could gaze at and wonder how you ever got so lucky just to be in it.

That night I made a promise to myself—a promise that at our Paris art opening, I would tell the world about Birch being the real artist. I was unsure how to do this, but hoped that when the opportunity came, I would just know. I fell asleep wondering how anything recognizes the perfect moment: how the tree knows it's time to fall or how the river knows it's time to branch. I wondered, as I began to dream, how a seed feels in the soil when it starts to grow.

That same night, unbeknownst to us, a shadow sneaked through the bushes outside Birch's studio. The shadow peered his beady little eyes through the window and watched Birch paint. "Aha," the shadow whispered. "I knew it. The boy is not the artist at all. It was the elephant all along."

The shadow was, of course, the Ringleader in all his dastardly, ghastly sneakiness. He twisted the points of his mustache and smiled his crooked yellow smile. "It's time to get back what's rightfully mine!"

FIFTEEN
A Beret and a Cupcake

"Wake up, wake up, time to wake up, my boys!" It was Slim Spatucci and he was right. If we didn't hurry, we'd miss our plane to Paris.

Once we settled onto our chartered transport plane and took off, I realized I would not miss Hollywood, with its fancy glamour and fancy people. I looked out the window of the plane and watched the heat lightning flashing in the distance. Every few seconds the whole world would light up, as if a giant were taking pictures of the neighborhoods and hills.

"Well, I'll be," I said. "Even the buildings want their photo taken in Hollywood."

I liked the way Paris looked from the air. The Eiffel Tower is tall, and at night they light it up and it looks like a ride at an amusement park, one where you might slide down its curved sides, laughing all the way and yelling *"Bonjour!"* to the air and, eventually, to the ground.

When we reached our room on the top floor of our hotel, I looked down at the crowds. Opening the window, I saw that the street below was crawling with head-tops resting upon suits and skirts, sliding in and out of cafés and shops; they looked like animals foraging for croissants and baguettes. An old man sipping espresso at a café on the corner looked up and saw me at the window, thinking, maybe, that I was going to jump.

"Excuse me," I yelled down. "Have you seen a beautiful acrobat?"

The old man smiled a broad, misinterpreting smile. "Silly Americans," he said, and laughed.

"Birch," I said, "how on earth are we ever going to find her? This city is full of people, and we don't even speak French!"

Birch, who had been taking a meditation yoga class back in Hollywood, had his eyes closed and was doing some sort of stretch. He took a deep breath. "Have faith," he told me.

"Maybe if you just relax, she'll find us." Birch closed his eyes again and started to hum, "Ohhhhhm," he chanted. "Ohhhhhm. Ohhhhhm. What we need is to get our minds off it for a while," he continued. "I've got an idea. Why don't we go out and see a bit of the city?"

And so we put on our berets and ventured out onto the Paris streets. Birch's hat was too small for him, and he looked the way I would look if I decided to wear a cupcake on my head. I couldn't understand what most of the people around us were saying, since they spoke French, but much like listening to birds chattering to one another or dogs howling at night, it was a lovely feeling to hear strange words.

It was a peaceful day. As we walked through a park, I saw bees bowing inside flowers to collect nectar. I watched as squirrels turned their paws purple eating berries and a dog stuck his nose inside a fallen wasp's nest, only to run away a moment later. Everything seemed to be looking for the sweetest part of the world. Birch did this too, stopping in his tracks every time he saw a woman wearing bright red or orange.

"Is that Dahlia? Is that the acrobat?" I'd say. But no, it never was.

Later that afternoon we signed up for a private walking tour of the city. Our guide had a face like the body of an old cow, all angles and crags and shadows. "*Pardonnez-moi*," he said, "but you two gentlemen look awfully familiar."

"We've been on TV," I told him.

"*Non*, don't watch TV."

"We've been in magazines."

"*Non*, don't read magazines."

"And newspapers."

"*Non*, don't follow newspapers."

"We were in a zoo for a while."

"*Non*, don't know much about zoos. Art," he said. "I really love art. I know I'm just a lonely tour guide without much in this world, but ever since I was a boy, I just loved looking at art."

"Well, we're sort of artists too," I said.

The man's face lit up. "*Oui*, that's exactly how I know the two of you. You're the painter boy who lives on an elephant's back. I've got a celebrity on my tour today."

"You want to know a secret?" I said. "Birch is the real painter."

"Well, that's not too surprising," the guide said. "A painting comes from what's in the heart, and elephants have mighty big hearts."

"And this week," I said, "Birch is having his Paris art debut. Want to know another secret? He's hoping that the acrobat he loves will come to the show, find him, and fall in love with him too." Birch blushed.

When the guide dropped us in front of our fancy hotel after the tour, Birch offered to give him a painting lesson. The concierge found a few sheets of paper and Birch rustled up some old paints, but in our mess of luggage we couldn't find a paint-brush.

"You can use my tail," Birch told him. It worked too. An elephant's tail looks a lot like a paintbrush. Birch taught the old man how to layer the colors and how to see the shades of light in the world and then how to translate them onto the page. He told him that you don't have to paint the world how everyone else sees it. You can paint the world how you see it. They are both the truth. You paint what defines a feeling for you and you alone—a color, an angle, a dash of the brush. The man finished a whole painting before he had to go. It was a picture of a yellow dress, his mother's favorite from her younger years, dancing in the wind on a clothesline. He said that one gust of air moving that yellow cotton dress defined the feeling of his whole childhood.

"Not a lot of elephants would let you use their tail to paint a picture," the man said. "I felt black and white today, but the two of you colored me in."

SIXTEEN
Postcards

[In a postcard (from Pigeon to the residents of the too-small-for-a-name town) that has a picture of the Musée des Égouts de Paris.]

THIS IS A MUSEUM ABOUT THE VAST SUBTERRANEAN WORLD OF SEWERS. IT IS STRANGE. WHEN WE TOOK THE TOUR THEY TOLD US IF IT RAINS, THEY'VE GOT 30 MINUTES TO GET EVERYONE OUT BEFORE THE TOUR AREA FLOODS.

PIGEON

[In a postcard (from Pigeon to Darling Clementine) that has a picture of a shop called Deyrolle on rue du Bac. It's a tiny place, a taxidermy shop.]

AT THIS SHOP, NO ANIMAL IS TOO EXOTIC, OR TOO ORDINARY, TO
BE STUFFED. LIONS, TIGERS, A CHIMPANZEE, A KANGAROO, A
WARTHOG. SOME ARE ONLY FOR DISPLAY, BUT SOME ARE FOR
RENT OR FOR SALE. JUST THINK: YOU COULD HAVE A ZEBRA AT
YOUR NEXT BIRTHDAY PARTY.

PIGEON

P.S. THEY ALL DIED OF NATURAL CAUSES.

[In a postcard (from Pigeon to Mama and Papa) with a picture
of the Chapelle Expiatoire on the front. This postcard has no
address.]

THIS IS WHERE LOUIS XVI AND MARIE-ANTOINETTE WERE
LAID TO REST AFTER THEY WERE GUILLOTINED. IT IS A
MAGICAL, HAUNTED PLACE IN THE HEART OF PARIS.

PIGEON

[In a postcard (from Pigeon to the Amazing Singing Hoboes)
that has a picture of a music festival called Fête de la Musique
and a crowd of musicians on the street.]

THIS IS A FESTIVAL WHERE AMATEURS AND PROFESSIONALS
SING AND PLAY IN PUBLIC SPACES ALL OVER FRANCE. JUST LIKE
YOU, BUT WITH MORE MEMBERS OF THE BAND.

PIGEON

[In a postcard (from Pigeon to Pierre the Turtle) that is colored
pure black.]

THIS IS A RESTAURANT CALLED DANS LE NOIR. YOU EAT IN
THE DARK AND ARE SERVED BY BLIND WAITERS. KIND OF LIKE
BEING INSIDE A SHELL.

PIGEON

[In a postcard (from Birch to his acrobat) that has on it a picture of the Louvre Museum.]

I LOVE YOU TILL THE END.

BIRCH

SEVENTEEN
A Wolf in Frog's Clothing

The art opening in Paris was very fancy. The gallery filled with fancy people in fancy clothing. The men wore black tuxedos and the ladies shimmering dresses, with diamonds in their ears and around their necks. Everyone listened to fancy music that tinkled through the air from the grand piano, and even the food was fancy: tiny mushrooms filled with heavenly cream and puff pastries oozing with crab served on fancy silver trays by fancy waiters.

Birch was nervous and paced back and forth in the gallery. He had on a bow tie and a top hat and looked quite dapper. Slim Spatucci gave us a thumbs-up and went out and told the piano player to stop playing. This was the moment I had been waiting for.

"Birch," I whispered, "are you ready?"

"Ready?"

"Ready for me to tell the world that you're the real painter." Birch was shocked, but managed to nod his head. I could feel his body tremble with joy.

"Your attention, please," I shouted. "I've got an announcement to make about our identity."

The crowd chattered excitedly. Birch smiled as he thought of the acrobat and floating with her in a bubble of love. The announcement meant more to Birch than anything had in a long time.

"Please be quiet," I said.

Birch held his breath. The room grew silent. It was so silent that you could hear a fly tapping its head against the window. "Do you mind?" I asked, and the fly sat still and was quiet.

"You are all here," I said, reading from the speech I had written, "because you are fans of me, Pigeon Jones, the boy wonder artist who resides on the back of an elephant. Well, there's something you all need to know."

"That's right, there is something you should know!" a voice

shouted from the back of the room. A man stepped forward wearing a frog suit.

"That boy is my son!" he shouted.

I dropped the pages of my speech and they fluttered to the ground. Birch said nothing, but in his heart, the hope he had felt at everyone knowing the truth burst like a bubble. It was as if my small hands, the same soft hands he'd held when I was a baby, had done the bursting.

I stared and stared at the man, then finally asked, "But how? How did you know where we were?"

"I read about you in the paper. My son, the famous artist. I've been searching for you forever."

"Papa?" I said, unsure. "Is it really you?"

"Of course it is. Look, I'm wearing my old frog suit."

Birch walked toward the man slowly, carefully, and leaned down. I stared at Papa and he stared at me.

I didn't recognize him, but then again I'd been so young when they left me at the orphanage. I stared harder. Yes, something about his eyes did look familiar.

"But where's Mama?" I asked.

"Why, she's away with the traveling circus troupe, but she will be back soon," he said.

"Is that where you've been?" I asked. "The circus?"

"Yes, we had to, Pigeon. We set out to make a life again in the circus. We were always going to come back and find you."

I leaned down and hugged Papa. His twisted mustache tickled my cheek. "And now I've found you," Papa said. "And you can finally join the circus with me."

"I've always wanted to join the circus!" I shouted.

"Wonderful!" Papa said. "You and your elephant are quite famous. You'd be a real draw for the crowds." The guests in the gallery cheered, and a few women dabbed their moist eyes, tearful about the touching father-son-elephant reunion.

I asked Birch to rush to the hotel so we could start packing. As we turned to leave, Slim Spatucci shouted, "Where do you think you're going?"

"Slim," I yelled with excitement, "it isn't every day that a boy finds his long-lost father!"

At the hotel we threw my belongings in a suitcase. Birch cleared his throat. "Pigeon, I think there's something suspicious about that man who says he's your father."

"What do you mean, 'says he's my father'? He is my father. You saw him—he's wearing a frog suit."

"Right," said Birch, "but there's something very familiar about him. I don't think he's who he says he is underneath that frog suit. That twisted mustache, the way he scuttles like a crab, even his voice. If I had to say, he reminds me a lot of the evil Ringleader."

"Why can't you be happy for me, Birch?" I asked. "I finally found my real family."

We didn't speak for the rest of the evening. How dare he say those things about my papa? While I brushed my teeth, I did ponder what he had said about real things hidden behind not-so-real ones. Mama had hidden behind her beard and Papa behind his frog suit in the circus. And then there was me. A lot of real things were hidden from me. I didn't know what a real bed felt like or what sitting at a dinner table felt like and, saddest of all, I had no idea what grass felt like underneath my toes. I could picture it, though. In my dreams my foot is dangling, shivering, stretching. I cling to Birch and dig my fingers into his back. I close my eyes and move my foot an inch closer to the ground. Closer and closer still. I can feel the warmth of the sun stored up in the soil. And then there's a soft breeze, barely perceptible, just enough to stir leaves and long blades of grass. One blade tickles my big toe. A small thing, to be sure, but I know I've never felt anything like it, never felt anything quite so real. I wondered if I ever would.

EIGHTEEN
Sometimes the World Is Littered with Peanut Shells

The circus was magnificent. There were brightly colored striped tents, and in the center ring a man held a stick in front of his face, blew on it, and breathed fire from his mouth like a dragon. To our left, a lion tamer got closer and closer to a lion, eventually holding its jaw and placing his head inside. Tiny drops of lion drool dripped in and tickled the inside of the man's ear, but he didn't flinch, which was probably a good idea. Children and parents packed into the tents, and the toddlers cried and laughed, wiping their tears with fingers sticky from cotton candy.

"And now," the announcer shouted, "in our center ring we present the world's largest artist and the world's pickiest art critic!" The spotlight came on, and Birch and I stood in the center ring beside an easel with a canvas and a palette. The canvas was very tiny. Birch wore a black-and-white-striped shirt, a red scarf, and a beret. I wore a three-piece suit and puffed on an unlit cigar.

"Paint! Paint!" I shouted. My role in the circus act was to play an art critic. Birch painted the first canvas, and then I shouted, "Bigger! Bigger!" And so a clown would bring out the next canvas, bigger than the last. This went on until Birch was painting a canvas as big as an elephant.

The paintings were awful—not real art like Birch usually painted, but circus art. There were pictures of clowns and dancing poodles. I thought Birch would be happy that I was happy, but he wasn't. Instead he seemed sad all the time. His ears drooped, his tail drooped, and his trunk drooped too.

When we finished our act, the lights went black and the crowd cheered. When the roar stopped, I heard a voice from the shadows. "Psssst!" it said. "Psssst! There's something I need to tell you."

"Who's there?"

"The man in the frog suit is not who you think he is," the voice whispered ominously.

"What do you mean?" I asked, starting to feel a bit faint. "He's my father."

"He's an imposter. He tricked you and your handsome elephant friend to perform in the circus."

Just as she said this, the lights came on and two thugs came around the corner and grabbed the owner of the voice. She was the most beautiful woman I'd ever seen, and she was dressed in all reds and oranges like a great plumed bird.

"Let go of me," she shouted, and struggled, but it was no use.

"It's her," Birch whispered, backing away.

"Her who?" I asked, but then stopped,

remembering all the paintings of red and orange birds Birch had painted. "The acrobat you loved," I whispered. Birch nodded, turned, and ran out of the tent.

Birch and I spent the remainder of the evening behind a Dumpster, sharing a bag of peanuts for dinner and trying to hatch a plan. Around Birch's feet was a soft blanket of discarded shells, and as he paced back and forth it sounded like we were trudging our way through a forest of dead leaves.

"We must save her!" he pronounced bravely as an accordion

player started playing in the distance. "But how?" he said as the music became sadder and sadder. I was upset as well. I didn't know what the acrobat meant when she said Papa wasn't who he seemed. Doubt and darkness crept into my heart.

I thought about our time on the train. Beancan Bill's talking aluminum can had given me some advice. He had said that when things seem the darkest, sometimes that's when you can see things the clearest. When he was a young bean can, he got opened, eaten up, and thrown in a gutter. He told me that for the first time in his life, he was so close to nothingness he could see the stark, aluminum anchovy-gleam of the world for exactly what it was; he could see what remains when idealism goes away. He said the world still looked pretty magnificent. Even from that gutter, if he turned the right way he could still see the stars in the sky, and he knew he'd always be all right, no matter what.

"Well, we're not getting anything done behind this Dumpster," Birch said.

We walked to our tent, marching to the lilt of the accordion music. I pondered the steps we had taken along the road of our adventure. Hopped a train, liberated a zoo, lived in Hollywood,

conquered the art world, ventured to Paris, joined a circus—
and now we had witnessed a potential kidnapping. It was a lot
to take in.

"It's gone," Birch said when we entered our tent. He was
frantically looking under blankets and chairs with his trunk.
"My paints and canvases, and all the money we made from the
art! All of it!"

Boy, were we blue. Usually Birch and I were a team, and
when one of us was feeling down, the other would shout, "Some-
place, there are trees full of sparrows. Somewhere, the trees
are singing." But not this time. This time we both stayed sad
and angry. I wondered if joy, like us, is a traveler and can't ever
stay put in one place for too long.

NINETEEN
The Triumphant Return of the Bumbling Pigeon

Birch narrowed his eyes and marched like an elephant on a mission toward the man in the frog suit's office. I'd never seen him like that before. He was dashing. He was valiant. He became the moment before thunder when the sky turns indigo and only the treetops dare to move and chatter.

He didn't even bother to knock when we stormed right into the tent.

"Where is she?"

"Where is who?" the Ringleader asked, twisting his mustache between his fingers. The frog suit lay on the floor. Birch and the acrobat had been right—the man in the frog suit hadn't been my papa. It had been the evil Ringleader all along.

"You know exactly who we're talking about," I growled.

"Oh, fine," the Ringleader said. "Here she is."

Two bulky guards brought the beautiful acrobat in from behind the tent. She pushed them away and ran to Birch.

"It doesn't matter," the Ringleader continued. "Dahlia signed a contract with the circus. And you, Birch? Well, you belong to me." He motioned to the guards, and they grabbed Birch by his ears.

"And to prove I still own you, I'd like you to go wash the clown cars just like you did when you worked at my car wash."

The guards put a bucket of water in front of Birch and laughed.

"All right," I said. "As a matter of fact, Birch and I have seen some dirty things around here that need cleaning." Birch leaned over the bucket and   filled   his trunk with water. Then he aimed his trunk right at the Ring-leader and sprayed water with the force of a circus cannon.

Everyone laughed. The beautiful acrobat's laugh sounded like mice tap-dancing on a xylophone, and Birch's laugh sounded like a bear tap-dancing on a bass drum. My laugh sounded like a pig snorting, and even the guards laughed. They sounded like someone trying very hard not to laugh.

"You don't own Birch and you don't own her," I said when the laughing was done. "And we're all leaving."

"Fine," the Ringleader said. "That's fine, you can all just go and leave me here alone." His mustache was wet and fell down his chin like a clown's frown.

"Leave me. I deserve it," the Ringleader cried. "I deserve to be alone. I'm garbage. Garbage, garbage, garbage. That's me, garbage!" he shouted.

Someone was listening to the Ringleader. Someone heard his cries. Someone came flying and bumbling into the tent. It was our old friend the pigeon, lover of garbage and all things yucky. The pigeon stared lovingly at the Ringleader and tilted her purple head to the side. She then waddled her fat body over to the Ringleader and gracelessly flew up to his shoulder, where she began cooing and rubbing her head against his neck, ear, and face.

"Git," the Ringleader said. But the pigeon would not go.

"Git," the Ringleader said, but the pigeon only loved him harder.

"Git," the Ringleader said, but didn't really mean it.

The Ringleader recognized a part of himself in the bird on his shoulder. Many people only saw a fat, clumsy, dim-witted garbage-eater when they looked at a pigeon, but from up close, the Ringleader saw something else. He saw the emerald green feathers of the pigeon's neck rivaling those of the peacock; the way the shades of gray start dark at the head and fade lighter and lighter across the body like the sky over the sea; her eyes each a drop of honey at the tip of a spoon. The Ringleader got up close and saw that like him, like anything, this pigeon deserved to be loved.

"Stay," he said, and so the pigeon stayed.

The Ringleader finally filled the hole inside himself, the one he'd been trying so hard to fill with meanness and revenge. There are openings all around us: in the walls, the trees, the sky, and our lives. The goodness knocks softly, doesn't even glance at its watch, and just waits for the heart to open the door.

Before we left, the Ringleader gave us back our money and possessions, but swore he hadn't stolen anything. "I was afraid thieves might rob you," the Ringleader said. "I was just keeping your things safe." Birch winked at me, and then shook the Ringleader's hand with his trunk. The Ringleader blushed red and smiled at such elephant-sized forgiveness.

"Well," Birch said to Dahlia as we stood by the gates to the circus. "I guess this is goodbye. We can't stay here. Pigeon needs to be home where it's calm. He needs to go back to school. He needs . . . me."

"Oh," she said. "I understand." They both looked as if they wanted to say more, wanted to hold out the one dazzling green leaf that held the truth. Instead, the moment passed, and the leaf began to yellow, curling in on itself like the tip of a genie's shoe.

"Goodbye, good, kind Birch," she said, and softly kissed the front of his trunk.

I cried that night for the loss of my papa, even though I had never actually found him. I cried until I got the hiccups. Birch got me a glass of water and rubbed my back until I felt safe, as always, like a bird in a tree's branches. I realized that Birch had given up Dahlia for *me*. She was a dazzling phoenix, but, like the Ringleader's, Birch's heart belonged to a silly pigeon.

Birch and I turned and began the long walk to the docks and the boat that would take us home. I thought about direction. I thought about the Ringleader. I thought about how a man can get turned the wrong way and be stuck there. Sometimes he needs something big to change that. And sometimes he just needs a fat bird to perch on the rusty weather vane of the heart and spin it in a different direction.

TWENTY
L'Art de la Mer

The next morning at dawn, Birch and I reached the coast of France, where there was a bustle of activity. As the first light appeared, the brown darkness collected in cabinets and corners and pockets. Cars, bikes, and people loaded on and off the large boats, and in between these behemoth vessels, smaller fishing boats docked to unload the early morning's catches. Men in black rubber boots tidied up their nets and turned their attention to the sea. The scent of phantom fish sneaked up to our noses, diving in and out of a soft breeze. Birch looked concerned as we watched from behind a fish truck. A man checked passengers' tickets as they boarded a transatlantic boat with the name *L'Art de la Mer* on the side.

"'Art of the Sea,'" Birch whispered. "Fitting name, but that sign says no animals allowed."

"You aren't boarding as an animal," I replied, pleased with my own cleverness. "Didn't you see the *other* sign?" Birch followed my gaze to the boat and to a sign that read DAMES SEULE-MENT. Ladies Only.

Birch and I stood in line waiting to board the ladies' cruise ship. A French woman in a high-collared black dress was greeting everyone. She looked very serious and very fancy. I straightened the large hat on Birch's head.

"Now, walk like a lady," I told him. Birch tried to walk with lighter steps, like a lady, but it was hard. For one, he's an elephant. And two, he was wearing a dress.

"Nobody is going to believe I'm a lady," Birch said. "I'm wearing a tablecloth."

"You're wearing a dress," I corrected. I too was wearing a dress and wig.

"They're old ladies," I continued. "They probably can't even see that well."

"Is that rain?" we heard a few ladies say, putting their

palms upward and looking to heaven. The clouds saw this as an invitation, and poured buckets into their waiting hands. "Run! Our dresses will be ruined!" the ladies cried, and all rushed toward the boat. Birch and I took this opportunity, joined the scramble, and made our way onto the ship without notice. A woman standing next to us looked Birch up and down. "You're a big woman now, aren't you? Well, your little girl is very cute." She smiled, gazing up at me.

After the women had dried off, they mingled, gossiped, removed their white gloves, and ate dainty sandwiches. The room seemed a bit cramped, so Birch and I made our way up to the deck and waited for the ship to set sail.

As we stood and looked out at the sea, something caught my eye in the dark water. "Look, Birch," I said, pointing. "It's a sea turtle."

We watched the powerful black creature move effortlessly, like a bird, through the water. The sea held endless specks of twinkling mica, and all around the beast were lines of light radiating from the ocean floor. I wondered where the light came from, and then I heard it. Below the surface, below the temperate miles of blue-green water pierced with fish, below the darkening shades of jade, lay the ocean deep, where no light penetrates. But there is still life. A translucent shrimp, insignificant as air, moved. Its world was all darkness, so dark it couldn't tell when a giant turtle netted with light passed overhead. I could hear the taps of this shrimp's featherlike appendages as she danced across the ocean floor, over a bare, cratered land of plains and valleys, as her luminescence sent rays of light higher and higher.

The boat slowly picked up speed and pulled away from the dock. I felt like I was flying as I clung to Birch's back, listening to the ship's flag applauding in the wind. The boat ride was fairly uneventful for the next few hours. We fed French fries to the seagulls that dipped and dived above our heads like white china plates flung through the sky. We watched a school of tiny silver fish move through the water and under the boat like a great puff of smoke coming out of a factory and shifting through the air.

Our attention diverted from the world below when the weather above started to change. The sun tiptoed away and hid behind the horizon line of clouds. The rain started again and everyone left the deck for the shelter of the cabin, but Birch and I stayed out. We threw our heads back and laughed because, really, what's a little rain? It felt fresh, and I remembered what Birch had told me about one thing hiding behind another. I had taken a bath the day before, for example, but here I was taking another.

"Miss," a man's deep voice said behind us. "Miss?" I ignored him because I forgot, momentarily, that we were dressed like ladies.

"I'd like to have a word with you and your friend.

Something about you seems"—he paused—"very fishy." The voice belonged to a security guard.

"Why, whatever are you talking about?" I replied in a high-pitched voice, trying to sound as innocent as possible.

"What is *that*?" He spun around sharply and pointed his police baton at Birch's trunk.

"That's her nose. What are you trying to insinuate? That there's something wrong with this woman's *nose*? How rude."

"Fine. Well, then, what are . . . *these*?" the officer asked, resting his hand on one of Birch's tusks.

"Those," I said, "are her teeth. Is it a crime in this country to have an overbite?" The officer straightened his badge, breathed warm breath on it, and shined it with his sleeve. "You need to show me your tickets for the cruise," he continued. "Let me see those. I'm security on this boat. It's my job."

"We dropped them overboard when we were looking at the sea turtle."

"Well, then." He smiled. "It seems I'll have to take you ladies downtown when we dock. Law's the law. That is, if we can find a jail cell big enough for—" The officer stopped talking when something caught his attention out at sea.

"What in the world?" the officer asked, pointing. Birch and I squinted to see through the rain. To our shock, it was the sea turtle we had seen earlier sailing through the waves. And on her back, with feathers blazing like fire, rode Dahlia. The acrobat traveled with her back to the mid-morning sun, creating a halo around her and giving the strange caravan an otherworldly glow.

TWENTY-ONE
Beneath Our Feet

The turtle pulled up alongside the boat. Dahlia was wearing a now soaking-wet costume.

"What are you doing on that sea turtle?" I shouted.

"I needed to talk to Birch."

The acrobat and the elephant attracted the attention of the passengers, and a crowd gathered on deck.

The acrobat closed her eyes. "I love you, Birch," she said. "I always have. The embers of love never truly go out. If the weather is right and there's not too much rain and a wayward match is flung out a car window, well, in due time it may catch fire. It may catch and blaze yet again."

Birch tooted his trunk like a boat horn. "Toot, toot, *toooot!*" He tooted louder than I'd ever heard him toot.

The ladies on the ship all swooned and then clapped their hands. While there is a lot of romance in movies and books, we rarely get to see it in real life. The boat buoyed just a bit higher out of the water that day because of all the memories of love rushing into everyone's hearts, all the happy thoughts they started having about all the people *they* had loved, and all the ones who had truly loved them back, the ones who still paced the marble corridors of the heart waiting to be remembered, waiting to remind a forgetful soul of its true loveliness.

Two mates on the ship threw a life preserver overboard and then helped Dahlia climb a ladder onto the boat. Dahlia was wrapped in a towel and brought a warm cup of tea. Everyone on the ship was asking her a million questions. Birch and the acrobat hugged and smiled and whispered to each other, but I was more interested in the sea turtle still lounging beside the boat.

She was giant, bigger than any turtle I had ever seen in life or in books. Why, she was almost as big as Birch. And old. Very, very old. Birch once told me that painting was like seeing the world being created new each morning. Mountains rose slowly, yawning and stretching out of the ground. Rivers grew deeper and wider and began moving like trains, slow, then fast, and faster still toward the sea. The flowers in the meadow took their places like an attentive audience and watched the sky paint itself blue and the trees pin on each leaf. The world did feel very new every day.

But this turtle did not feel as if she were created new every morning. She felt very old, older than one day, older than time itself. Her shell was covered in barnacles and moss and fallen leaves, and I think I saw a sapling growing there as well. Smells of shadows and frogs' feet filled the air around her, and the sunlight had trouble pushing through all the ghosts to reach her shell. Yes, this was a very old creature. This was not created new every morning. Perhaps, I thought, the world had forgotten about her.

"Hello," I said.

"Hello," the turtle said in a deep voice.

"You're not like anything I've seen," I said.

"I'm a magical creature," she replied.

"Are you a unicorn?"

"No."

"A centaur?"

"No."

"A dragon?"

"No. I'm a very, very, very old sea turtle."

"Is that . . . magical?" I asked.

"Allow me to tell you a story," the turtle said. "You see, scientists have shown us how astronomy works: that the earth orbits around the sun and that the sun, in turn, orbits around the center of a vast collection of stars called our galaxy. However, a group of people called the Hindus believes that the world rests upon an elephant. And the elephant rests upon the back of a giant turtle."

"I've heard that story," I said. "But I always wondered what the turtle rests upon."

She paused. "Well, the Hindus would tell you, 'Something,

but we know not what.' And this is a wise notion, because we will never get to the bottom of things. We do not know what supports the turtle that supports the elephant that supports the world. No man stands on absolute truth. Perhaps we are merely banded together, each of us leaning on one another, keeping the world afloat."

I sat and thought about that for a moment, how each person has lots of people in his or her life, and how all those people make up the world for that person. Perhaps home is not located over mountains and through cities, past trains and tracks and across the ocean. Perhaps home is always right in our hearts and beneath our feet.

TWENTY-TWO

The Best Position There Is

When Birch, the acrobat, and I reached home, all our friends had gathered to greet us. All our neighbors were there and Slim Spatucci too. Even the Amazing Singing Hoboes were there. They sang with acrobatic fervor, bodies leaning, arching, on tiptoe at the high notes. I could hear the waves of song like flapping wings, traveling out, some snaking through and becoming trapped in the hairs on Birch's back, the rest falling softly, dancing through the wet grass.

"I had a dream," Pocketless Pete said. "I was in a garden and I saw a leaf fall from a tree toward the ground, only to be caught by another leaf on the same tree. It was a nice thing to see, and I figured it meant you were coming home."

While we were gone at the circus, Slim Spatucci had finished my announcement and told everyone in the art world that Birch was the real artist. The critics were even more excited about an artistically gifted elephant than about an artistically gifted boy. Slim was planning a world tour.

"I can't go on a tour," Birch said. "I can't go anywhere at all."

That's when I finally understood. As long as he had to care for me, Birch would never have a life of his own. He'd feel needed, but never be the great elephant artist I knew he could be.

"Birch," I said, "could you do me a favor?"

"Anything," he replied.

"Could you take me to the park?"

The park looked the same as I remembered it. The fence behind home plate was still standing at a strange angle and the grass in the outfield was much too long, the boys in shorts leaning over every few minutes to brush the flies from their legs. I watched a boy who lived down the street square up at bat and spit in the dirt. The sun was hot, and he squinted. I imagined as he focused on the ball everything else around it became a blur of sunburned faces and gangly limbs.

Two boys ran over to us and waved.

"Hey you," the one with freckles and a crooked smile said. "We need a shortstop. You play?"

"I'm a fan of baseball, yes," I said, stretching the truth a bit.

"Well, then, get down off your crazy ride and get out here. You can play short. Short's the best position there is." The boys ran back to the field and I stared at their backs getting smaller and smaller.

"Short really is the best position there is," a voice behind us said. I turned and there was Darling Clementine sitting on a fence, wearing a blue dress, and looking just as perfect as I remembered.

"Perhaps it's time to get down off your *Elephas maximus indicus*," Darling said. "I can't grab your big ears and kiss you hello if you're way up there."

I almost fainted. I did, in fact, want to kiss Darling Clementine. I had no idea what short was, but I wanted to be out there with those boys punching my fist into a sweat-stained glove. I knew it was time.

"Birch," I said, running my hand over his neck, remembering when I was a baby and felt his skin for the first time, rough as the bark on a tree. "Birch, I need you to give me something," I said quietly.

"I'd love to, Pigeon, but I don't know that I have anything left to give you," Birch replied. "I was old and retired when we met and now I'm even older still."

He was right. He was not as strong as he had once been. Caring for me had taken its toll on him. "Oh, I don't need much," I told him. "All I really need is for you to give me a hand getting down to the ground."

I didn't have to say anything more.

Birch leaned the front half of his body down and bowed his head. I took a deep breath and climbed up, up over his head and his ears and sat at the top of his trunk. Then I slid down, down, down toward the grass, and I felt the earth under my feet. Birch stood up proudly behind me.

"It's been an honor and a privilege," Birch said, bowing his head and closing his kind elephant eyes. I felt nothing but gratitude as I curled my toes into the grass and said, *"Thank you. Thank you. Thank you."*

TWENTY-THREE

Trout-Bellied Rainbow Skies

When Birch and Dahlia went on tour, I began a new life with my new adoptive family—our old circus friends in the too-small-for-a-name town. I slept in a bed instead of on an elephant's back. In the morning I ate breakfast in the kitchen, where the bacon made grease ghosts on the paper towels over the plate. I bathed in a bathtub instead of being sprayed by an elephant's trunk, and if the bathwater was hot enough, steam came off my skin afterward like mist on a lake in the night. I liked walking everywhere, and I never wore shoes.

"Take your shoes off," I told Darling Clementine when I went over to her house to play. "Now throw them out the window!" She did, and we walked over the gravel road, the dry grass, and the lake rocks covered in muck.

"Has it always felt like this?" she asked.

Still, sometimes I would get sad. Darling saw this and asked, "What's wrong?"

"Oh, nothing," I said. I went outside and looked at a sunset striped like a trout's rainbow belly. I thought of Birch and how he would have loved to see it and paint those colors.

"I've got a surprise," Darling said one afternoon. We got on our bikes and pedaled to the next small town. She took my hand and led me through the exhibits of a small zoo to a large enclosure with high fences.

"Elephants!" she said. "Look."

I looked and looked and tried to be happy. I didn't want to upset Darling. She was trying so hard to make this day special, but I couldn't help it. I felt my face and it was wet with tears.

"Pigeon, I'm sorry," said Darling. "I thought you'd like the elephants."

"I do," I said. "I do." That was the problem. They only reminded me of Birch. He had been my whole world for so long. His head had been a high hill sloping down the valley of his trunk. The hairs on his neck were spruce and shrub and his skin a dry riverbed, the cracks making a patterned mosaic.

129

And so I ran. My feet pounded against the dirt and carried me out of the zoo, into the woods, over a fallen tree, and out the other side. When I stopped I was at the edge of my own town. In front of me stood a makeshift house, which was really just a roof with three walls made from planks of wood off old circus train cars. The boards had pictures of animals painted on them—lion heads on hippo bodies and monkey feet attached to alligator smiles.

Nothing looked right. The rain and weather had faded the pictures and they were almost too faint to see. Some of the nails had rusted, and vines had started to grow up and separate the planks of wood.

"Birch?" I said. But of course nobody answered.

I walked back to the zoo, slowly, with my head down. It was starting to get dark, and when I turned the corner, Darling Clementine was there waiting.

"I stayed here in case you came back."

"Thanks," I said.

A tiny bird flew into the enclosure and landed on an elephant's back. The elephant didn't seem to notice. I realized time is like a small bird. If I could have caught it, I would never have had to grow up, would never have had to leave my childhood bedroom—Birch's back—the room with the greatest view. But I learned, as everyone eventually does, that tiny birds are nearly impossible to catch.

"Where did you go?" Darling Clementine asked.

"I tried to go back," I said. Darling was quiet. She just nodded knowingly, put her head on my shoulder, and stood with me watching the elephants until the zoo closed.

You use wood to build a boat, but it's in the space where there is nothing that the boat becomes useful. And we build a house, but it's on the open spaces, windows and doors, that the usefulness of the house depends. In the space after I left Birch's back, I discovered what it means to find someone who loves you, someone who will carry you when you need to be carried and let you go when it's time, finally, to be free.

TWENTY-FOUR

The Masterwork of a Painting Elephant

With his new career, shows, and interviews, Birch began to see his life as a busy garden filled with puddles of lovely rain. And he saw the acrobat as the moon. At night she glowed through his window and reflected in every pool. Hundreds of crescent moons, more than he could count, filled his world with light.

An elephant and an acrobat. No stranger than the owl and the pussycat, minus one pea-green boat.

The acrobat was by Birch's side when he was on the news and the cover of *Time* magazine. She was there when he met the president and first lady and gave them a ride around the White House. The acrobat traveled with Birch to his art shows, and there were many: in Milan, Venice, London, Tokyo, and Sydney. And, of course, in Paris, where they made their home.

In winter, as the snow danced and the wind whooped and cheered, Birch painted a picture of the Ringleader. He painted a bronze statue, tall and broad with a pompous posture. And on the shoulder of the statue stood pigeons, disfiguring the dashing figure. "I think it adds a needed air of humor," Birch explained. He also painted an old forest, with light sprinkling through the canopy and Spanish moss draped over branches. There, a set of wind chimes hung in an old tree. Rain and cold had made them rusty, so they echoed as if the forest were a temple and the chimes were locked far away in a tower. A great artist can capture sound on a canvas. This was his portrait of the Amazing Singing Hoboes.

By early spring water ran off the tips of icicles, and Birch covered his canvas in the most beautiful green color. A white rabbit could be seen hopping away and in the grass, where it had sat, there was a bunny indentation. The creature imprinted the grass just as Slim Spatucci had helped Birch imprint the world. "This one," Birch explained, "I dedicate to Slim."

In the summer the tree frogs sang in the night, and Birch created a picture of all the people in our too-small-for-a-name town. The picture showed the woods in early evening, when hundreds of fireflies glittered like children playing flashlight tag in a faraway land. Birch painted a pale, gauzy day moon over the town as a reminder that my parents, though gone, would never be forgotten.

And in fall, as the air buzzed with electricity, Birch walked along treelined streets. "The world is so beautiful," he whispered, "I can't concentrate to paint at all." I imagine the old elephant thought of me as he gazed up at the leaves above him. Long ago a man had planted those trees, arranging the seedlings in two evenly spaced rows, one on each side of the street. It took almost two centuries for the moss-draped branches to find each other again and meet overhead.

One night at the end of autumn, in some distant tower a clock chimed at midnight, then stopped. I heard a tapping at my window. When I got out of bed, the floor felt cold and the dark furniture looked like large, slumbering animals.

"Hello," I whispered out the window. "Hello?"

"Pigeon, is that you?"

"Yes," I said.

"It's me, Birch."

"Birch!"

"Look how tall you've gotten," Birch said when I stepped outside. He stood in the garden outside the house. The leaves on the trees were covered in holes left by hungry caterpillars and looked like demure doilies in the moonlight. Birch glowed among them. He looked older and smaller than I remembered, like a teacup made of china.

Birch set up an easel and paints. We stayed outside together for hours until Birch completed his final portrait. I began to wonder if it was all a dream until Birch said, "I am finished." He gripped the edge of the canvas. "It was a bit of a rush job, but yes, I do believe I've captured you, young man."

Birch held up the canvas, and there was a painting of me as a very tiny bird in the branches of a strong white birch tree.

"Yes, that's exactly how I see myself in my heart," I whispered.

I leaned against Birch and, for a brief and perfect moment, I was able to go back. Back to the day we met. Back to when my whole world rose and fell with Birch's breath and the sound of his heartbeat. My elephant was right about feelings of love: that they float away on the wind, circling the earth forever and landing, ever so briefly, from time to time. I understood then that I'd always be loved, always be safe, always be the one true masterwork of a painting elephant.

We sat together talking all night, watching the night flowers bloom, and listening to the stars converse with the moon. Birch had grown quite old, too old for the world. In my heart I knew that night would be the last I'd spend with my friend. When his time to go did come, I imagine Birch simply became part of the wind, and that the wind was happy to have him, weaving through the circus of time, strolling across the sea, lifting the wings of birds, and falling quiet at the close of day to ponder how morning breaks.